leni dipple

between rivers

OLDCASTLE BOOKS

First published in 2014 by Oldcastle Books,
P.O.Box 394, Harpenden,
Herts, AL5 1XJ, UK
oldcastlebooks.com

© Leni Dipple 2014

The right of Leni Dipple to be identified as the author of this work has been
asserted in accordance with the Copyright, Designs and Patents Act 1988.

A CIP catalogue record for this book is available from the British Library.

ISBN
978-1-84344-582-1 (print)
978-1-84344-583-8 (epub)
978-1-84344-584-5 (kindle)
978-1-84344-585-2 (pdf)

2 4 6 8 10 9 7 5 3 1

Typeset in 9.5pt Palatino
by Avocet Typeset, Somerton, Somerset TA11 6RT

Printed and bound in Great Britain
by CPI Group (Ltd), Croydon, CRO 4YY

for Siân and Corinne

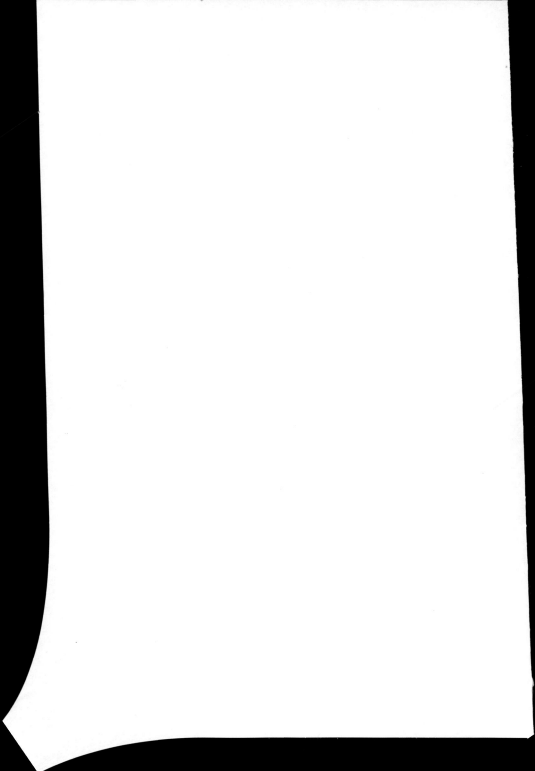

'Porque nasci entre espelhos
tenho pressa
de encontrar-me face a face'

from 'Os Espelhos' 1966–1967
Helder Macedo

CONTENTS

Preface

'to found new land from which men and women may speak'

Nearly all of these poems were written over an intense period spanning twelve years during which I struggled to learn my craft, find my voice and a self which had been overlaid with the suffocating culture of patriarchy in the calvinist Holland of my father. He was born in 1914 on the island of OverFlakkee, south of Rotterdam. By 1917 his mother had died of tuberculosis and his father, Jacob Koert, had re-married to Sara Gnirrep. She was a young independent woman who already held the position of matron in a hospital in Rotterdam. In a series of letters written to her by my grandfather during their brief courtship, I caught a glimpse of who he was and of his hopes for this second marriage. He had wanted an equal partnership with a modern woman who had already found an identity outside of marriage. He had taken the first steps to leave farming, the traditional occupation of his ancestors, and had gone into partnership to open a sugar beet factory on the island. Nonetheless, he was also the first farmer on OverFlakkee to use nitrate fertiliser to improve yields. A fact which probably contributed to his premature death of stomach cancer at the age of 51, in 1926.

When I started out on this journey, I too, was at a crossroads in my life and I looked to various guides for direction and spiritual support. I was reading Rilke and came across the stellar correspondence, *Letters: Summer 1926*, between himself, Marina Tsvetaeva and Boris Pasternak. These three voices all informed my writing at that time and I was struck by the parallel between my passion for the Portuguese language (Fernando Pessoa's poetry in particular) and Rilke's passion for all things Russian, which he felt to be crucial in the making of himself as a poet. It was only later that I realised the life spans of Rilke and my grandfather mirrored one another. Dante's journey also, spoke urgently to me at the outset of this quest. I too was lost in the dark woods of my middle years.

At the time of writing the poem 'origin' I had been struggling to re-define who I was as a wife, mother and perhaps, a poet; to attempt a new weave between these roles. I remember very well mentally addressing myself to the grandfather I had never met, but who had established a presence in my imagination through his letters to the woman I came to know as my 'Oma', my Dutch grandmother. From that point my journey became multi-layered in that I began to explore the physical and the metaphorical aspects of my roots. I discovered the house where my father was born on the delta of OverFlakee. The young couple living there spoke frankly to me about the very insular culture and the in-breeding which had resulted. How, being aware of this danger, they had independently left the island to seek new horizons, only to meet by chance in a discotheque in Utrecht. They had already fallen in love when they discovered shared family bloodlines which effectively vetoed their having children.

That evening of our meeting was one of the strangest of my life. They had bought the farmhouse from an uncle, who in fact had bought it from my grandfather's estate. Together we discovered the link in our family histories and together we took a lantern to visit the cemetery at the bottom of their garden to see if we could find my paternal grandmother's grave. It was a pitch black November night but I went straight to a grave and touched a tombstone. We were unable to read the inscription, so they returned the following day to clean the stone and found that indeed the grave was that of my grandmother. She has been a benevolent presence in my life ever since. Whenever I return to that part of the world I feel a kinship with the land which is tangible. And it is this sense of kinship, its energy, which asks to be articulated and translated, to find new 'land' literally and metaphorically. During the writing of these poems I travelled in my mind to another delta, that of Mesopotamia, the origin of writing, via Africa, the origin of our species.

Where was my mother in all this? When she married the stranger who had bought a patch of land, creating Eagle Nursery, near to her family farm in Essex she too had stepped outside the traditional pattern of her class and culture. It was a bold move and one which implied not just changing her name to 'Koert' but also surrendering her British nationality to travel to meet her in-laws on the same Dutch passport as her husband. That was how it was at that time. She had married an alien and in so doing she alienated herself within her own English culture. Nonetheless, something in her also needed to seek new horizons and perhaps this collection of poetry is for her, as well as for my daughters. It is written in my mother tongue, hers, because it is out of that dual source of a particular rooted language and her womb, that these poems have come to see the light.

And what of the father of my daughters? He too was a product of two cultures, the Welsh and the English and although his first language was the Welsh of his mother's side, he lost touch with it. I feel it was a tragic loss; to be Welsh speaking at that time was considered a handicap. But when his first daughter Corinne was born, he spontaneously, just the once, sang a Welsh lullaby. His life was one of struggle amid forces which always threatened to overwhelm him. He too died prematurely of cancer aged 51, a loss not only to his two daughters and me, but also to the world of jazz, where he had found his voice and a just recognition in our business 'Mole Jazz'.

I am writing this preface in a café in south west France where I've been living permanently since 2002. Three years before my husband's death I traded a stay in a small farmhouse, owned by an Englishman, for French tuition. We'd never considered a second home as an option, but this house with its tumbledown barn attached, cast a spell on me. A year after our stay the owner's business had failed and my mother had died of cancer. I bought the house and furnished it with my mother's furniture. Since that time I have been actively exploring the local culture; from troubadour poetry to working with my neighbours on the village committee, to creating an organic 'potager'. I belong to the WWOOF movement (wwoof.fr – 'world wide opportunities on organic farms') and am currently working on a new project built around the contributions made by the many wonderful *wwoofers* who come to share my life here and learn about sustainability in all its aspects.

Last but not least, my new home provides me with some distance from the all pervasive language of consumerism which has invaded Britain since Margaret Thatcher's era. You could say that my presence here is, to a certain extent, an exile from that mother tongue which feeds my poetry. But it's a challenge which I embrace in order to be true to that life force emanating from the 'land', both physical and metaphorical, of my ancestors and guides.

I

Life Palette
Estoril, 1980

'O sol é grande, cuem co'a calma as aves'
Sá de Miranda (1481–1558)

Perched on a sill I looked down
Saw shadows of birds on the sand
Unseen   they fly on high
Elusive reflections glimpsed

through the aura of Iberian
days and sun on scented pine
But life advanced no purchase
offered only the birds of Braque

Stove black
they flew from his hand
leaving cinders in the heart
the grate cold

And the pain of confinement
swooped down and perched
unseen   crowing
in my empty house

I feel its vacant stare

lollipop

with what slow intensity
she lifts the stick and then plunges it
into sand, her chosen spot
inside a neatly cordoned plot full
of sandy surprises at the school summer fête

the wooden tabs protrude like poking tongues
the tongues which once had licked and sucked
before the toothsome tang, the acidic, enamel-eating
stick-bleaching ice could melt

before my child's desire could melt
luminous orange lolly ice
painting lips and tongues together
digging deep for treasure

my ice-hoard
sifting like Psameadd and Wanderer
through sand shifting, sleep deep
searching for signs, mark-making
plunging tabs into time, trying
to recover and recognise the oar, the spine

when lickety split
down memory lane i
trundle out with doll's pram and baby
to visit the lolly man
a whole mile down the road
and my first purveyor of gold

under glass

i

in my mother's drawer
(her pandora's box
of making faces)
lies the silken blotter
perfumed and stained

the way-in to a changing room

when i press it softly to my lips
my first attempts at drawing outlines
slip onto her silk

shh mother's sleeping

tip toe tip toe
into the mirror

ii

press the blotter softly
to my lips
close my eyes
let it take me away

go to sleep won't you won't you

dropping down between my legs
gagging on your descent
oh hold the blotter to my lips
let it mask the outline
of your mouth

wanting more always more

iii

like your fag smoke
i clung on
knocking at doors
so hard in the night
my dreams dissolved into darkness

i built greenhouses to capture
the light
and every day under glass
felt the sun rise in your limbs
petal soft

knowing that every day
night would come

were you ever my wife?
were you ever my wife?

FATHER / land

Trying to substitute words
for apples is mad   Mad is
an apple signifying wind
streaming round and through me
A cold passion which kills

Now snapshots appear
between bare branches
They fall like leaves
from a family album
They sing of the wind's cold
kiss and fruitless marching
Of reunion and parting

Remember they whisper
remember the wind
biting through words
signifying the apple
baked into lies   and
the gas streaming
cold passion which kills

In Africa tom-toms
would beat   Would beat
the syllable out to ride
astride the thrum until
the drum be fat   Until
the core be raw   Open
the original apple   Eat!

playground

my skin, my playground
in which i'd swing higher and
higher, inviting you in

my skin, my playground
has ropes and slides
upon which your eye
would ride its own roundabout

my skin, my playground
wound round and round in laughter
until the ground rose up giddy
like a skirt spun out

and we fell down, down
we fell down

left-handed

I am in the kitchen cooking quiches
gross feeders circling all around me.
Dear Lorca is lying open on my table
with his lemons and oranges piled high
by the sink. I pick up my knife,
I'm doing the onions, cut a slice
of lemon and run it down the blade;
acid on steel takes the taint away.
Then I cradle the tin and cut through
the limp pastry. The floury folds
fall away from the rim.

Singing lullabies to Lorca, I dance
in my kitchen. Stave off my hunger
for delicate forms. What shall I do
with the remaining pastry?
There's enough left over for something
sweet. Roll it up and bake it, fill
it with fruit, sprinkle with sugar
and tonight, for a treat, I'll rise
with the moon as it turns to honey,
just behind my left shoulder, discrete.

ignition

alight
in the black taxi
ridden to devour
the silver lining
of a throng
lighting tapers
in the Strand

and the black steeds
eat coal
which is wet
from the rain
driving hard
down the Strand

I offer silver...
'keep the change'
make a light
exit

Pointer

"Alfred had me made"
Aelfred mec heht gewyrcan

maker's hands first
held me, drew my snout
down to align his eye
in true conjunction
with the fine tool
from which i grew

he gave me his eyes
so others might feast
upon my perfect form
when, fixed like flies
on a corpse in the sun
i lead them by the nose

flairing the way
through word and *burh*
from cover to cover

I make my point
on the high ground
of Alfred's England

'Frelater'

How does your fine tool
spend his days my friend?

I lift my glass
to his obsolete form,

take another sip
of the house *pinard*

and think of France
A rich conversation

with friends about *'frelater'*
and just how it translates.

Is it 'to spoil'
or is it 'adulterate'?

In my cups I slip,
let the glass drop.

The bulb sheers off
from its stem.

I squat to pick up
this prick of a life.

Its blood dribbles out
on my hem.

therapy

seeing you
in that cell
my lost sixteen years
cleaned out by mother's
sun-bloated evacuation

seeing you
in that cupboard
which housed my toys

i have to pay to go there

and i only allow myself
a fixed term, twice a week
for precisely one hundred and ten
minutes, equally divided

between my self and that other
you   and my mother
and we're not allowed to touch

you want me in that cupboard
you need to have me, right there –
i go willingly, with a mute stare, hating
the wanting of this fuck by proxy

this emptying by penetration
of the delicate membrane
which has become too light
sensitive a shield

for this world's crucial
commerce in soul-trading

The Ballad of Zé and Marie
(or a Rodeo in the House of Commons)

I've come in from Vigo
stabled my pony in the hold,
picked up my guitar
and a nugget of gold.

I've come in from Vigo
by river and by ferry.
I could see no light
but the white city prairie.

Coming down by river,
it felt good – promising
fresh snow, a deep pile
carpet. And offering

hope for an old cod
to strike his match
in a tight, white cowboy
suit. I'll cut a dash

in the clothes we first
dated in. My heart
knows her, but will she
recognise an old fart

in a time-earned disguise –
with belly slung low,
his guns at the door,
whose draw's a mite slow?

I rescued the pony.
She was cold from standing.
Tuned my box, tied my bolo
for a turquoise landing.

Close to the house
my voice is mum, failing
inside I hear her waves
of laughter breaking

on an unknown beach
and, hard as an edge
in between two worlds,
I drive my wedge.

II

the house is full now, the benches packed
i sit expectant and recollect a white petticoat
edged with lace which clung to my slight form
snow fell outside, it was indoor play

my dress was plain oh how i craved beauty
so i took it off and felt real pretty
in my white nylon petticoat, edged
with pretend lace

it was i who asked
marry me, i said, and you put on
your tight white cowboy suit
and he did

we made it there and then, kneeling on the bed
i seven and he eight

III

last night i washed my petticoat
out and hung it to dry
on the small indoor line in my flat

i cleaned up my buckskins they've come
back in fashion
and polished my black high-heeled boots

my hair is tied fast with a silver pin
carved like a fish with turquoise eyes
it pays to keep it almost hidden
in this love city where fear tips
the scales and glistens
tonight under snow

IV

The night of the Rodeo
The biggest Happening in the West
since God slipped Madonna a dollar that night

We're going to bring the House down
our pride blown like JFK's brains
on the backs of our buggies
We are riding dead broke into town
to the chimes of Big Ben
and there'll be no midnight striking
this Ball will go on and on
with all the TV cameras of the world
fixed like flies on the corpse
of our nation

all day long the undertaker's been pocketing
readies to line his Coffin
while his Assistant struggles
to make-up minds starved
on the Never Never   False Leads
No Direction

V

her pointer...

seek him   mark the spot
where prince glendower dances
the cavalier in cowboy suit

combine   this night   to weave a spell
with eyes like peacocks   blue and gold
to rescue me from the serial life
and save our children's story
from the fire which flickers cold
where there should be heat

stay in the circle   here
take his glove stuck with my pin
seek boy   seek   go seek!

VI

Isis, anyone for Isis?

off the leash, the dog bounds
his huge eyes burn like coals
made from forest power invested
and shored up for tonight's grand
stoking   his 'grande gueule'   the hopper
which steams breath   firing his limbs
feeding his snout with scent
the huge eyes burn blind as he runs
swift as a river between its banks
blind to the benches littered
with bitches' dancing
his lady's token intact

the Speaker sees him and circles
a lasso over his head but trips
catching his own foot instead

strange rodeo in the House tonight

he stops   poised
one leg raised   muzzle pointing

the glove falls
time to close the curtains

Hey Sister, got a light?

VII

Epilogue

they left the House by water
not scared but fighting shy
of the life ahead

'Turn round and let me see you'

and she swivelled on the heel of her boot

'i've maybe changed since the days
when I cradled your head   gun shy
from the africa war   you'd start
every time i touched you'

'Every time I touched you
I felt you running through my hands
like sand on the beach'

'divided loyalties –
do your kisses still taste of the sea?'

'Sure babe'

'is the valmar café still open
in vigo?'

'Sure babe   and still serving
the best coffee in the West'

walking through amsterdam

and waiting for the naming
of things

running my mind's eye
over their surfaces
they seem to be circular
and slip away to evaporate
like sea-spray on my skin

waiting for the naming
of things

crystallize the pearl
and allow it to be found
within its hard casing

my children are sleeping
dreaming of the naming
within their own day's
safe-keeping

they are dreaming
of the naming of things

II

Maas / Meuse / Muse

from the Haute Marne in France to the island of
OverFlakkee in the Netherlands

How do our great rivers impact upon us? The mystery
of their flow follows age-old rhythms, constantly
bringing us back to centre, to our heart.

And you, oldest of all rivers, suddenly speak; make
yourself known to me. Your story goes back long
before life began. You witnessed its greatest extinction
and then its regeneration; felt the first heart-beats in
your flow.

I pore over maps and discover your source in France.
Trace your course north west until you reach the
coast of the chill North Sea. Here your waters divide
into two arms cradling a land-fragment, the island of
OverFlakkee.

This ancient marriage between the oldest of all rivers
and a few thousand hectares of earth, caught in a
tug-of-war between land and sea, is where my father's
family farmed for generations.

origin

*in memory of my grandfather, Jacob Koert, 1875–1926
and my guide, Rainer Maria Rilke, 1875–1926*

i have written your names
underlined them

we all have beginnings
but christ   how it's hard to start

picture the unfinished painting
the swallow   root palace
both cradle and ark

i have to be wholly present

patient
in love like the first time
recover lost language

of my country's heart

diaspora

'But every fifty years or so
someone tears himself away
from family and farm
and goes in search of the edge'.
                              Vicki Feaver

my dad was the first
koert to go – not in fifty but
in five hundred years
how the earth's body churned
tore   stank at his defection
his passage over water
a solitary struggle   his wake
cut through like a knife

koert blood leached out
fear lapped at our land
under the hammer   guilt rode
on the back of debt fired by
the action and the spectacle
of a family's dis-memberment
in a classic dutch auction.

with a patriarch gone
the sun shone for the first
time in half a millennium
on what had been covered
so long   kept hoarded
it engendered mutations
a new thrust towards light

Oma
Sara Koert Gnirrep 1891–1976

suffer the solace
of my touch
on your tablecloth

the cover it offers
my smaller surface
affords a full surplus

it falls in folds
like your ample skirts
fell, to encircle and protect

my growing in your eye
i never saw your legs!
but clung to every word

tasted my father's tongue

caught crumbs of speech
half understood   made potent

by the laying-on
of hands on silver
in rank order   posed

for grace   hands
lifting for the surrender
of cup to lip

in absence of your sight
i witness absolution

the nurseryman's daughter

i am your girl-child
the one you feared, skirted
round, egged on
to take the first bite

now i'll rib you –
how you mistook my kiss
for the hiss of your own
tongue flickering to meet

mine – how we pretended
i could hide behind
a leaf… counting up to ten,
i promised i wouldn't peek…

if you would only find me!

The Dutch and Dentists

damn brown rice! my tooth
is broken   the grit of life
greedy for disrepair distraction
it comes in creeping through
the hair-line crack

my defences down words well
up from a water-logged land
i can taste the sand feel
the suction as he squirts air
i see my father in the chair
refusing an injection prior to
extraction and he
breaking out in a sweat

the dutch are familiar
with decay and damp   their houses
require special under-pinning
so why not accept dentures
a new set of pearlies
integrate distraction thought with
emotion   spit the grit out   in holland
the tradition of painting is strong

i practise breathing
as taught in ante-natal classes
and allow my mind to run free
through the dunes (i used to build
beautiful sandcastles)
while he works around my mouth

he knows my shade
allows for life's discoloration
i am colour coded A3
in this segment of life's orange
architect of teeth
will you renovate me?

for Serge Gainsbourg
(after 'Dieu est un fumeur de Havanes')

I love your songs of smoke
formless fluidity wrung
into taut wreathes worn
in your absence   Young

you looked more elf than man
A shy transformer of the base
into sheets of leaf silver
tapped from the symbiosis

of your art and women   Outré
consummation   like Dad's Dutch
cigars held my peace in blue
rings   puffed between lips with

such precision they circled
my form exactly   I loved
to light up for him play
in his smoky haze   Serge

I know how the hammer must
have hurt Just how much smoke
do we have to swallow before
our lungs are soot   before

we are consumed   hollow?

Perspective with Matisse
(The Piano Lesson, 1916–17)

step outside   look
beyond the railings   and listen
for hoofbeats the heart answers

i'm stuck with madame's metronome
for the duration   but you …

if only she could see your reflected shadow
slanting across my face

off centre, you excite

would your warm tones sound
for me like ivory keys?
africa   oh africa (i need your touch)

she perches back there, stiff old parakeet
umpiring my play
back and forth   back and forth
a song framed by scrawniness, plumage shed

i'm sure she needs to scratch, has fleas

come with me to africa   do
ride bareback down the green strip
out of the picture completely

oh god   why must my eye
travel back   snarl in wrought-iron
circle the delicate whorl   the loop
winding unwinding re-winding

memory in pink on piano top

Meditation for M. on a Self-Portrait

i

How the picture harbours peace;
each shape, each colour line my eye.
Do you believe in the indelible?
You realise the light's too bright
(practically Mediterranean) attend
to it directly. Drop a shutter,
douse it. Your relief deepens with
the shade. I do not dare to dip
myself entirely in the angle between
beret and eye, respect what it may
signify. Forgive me M. if I feel
the raw selvage. May I try to work
a hem?

ii

       i used to sew
                 while swans flew over
mute, with sore fingers
             from the flax
now i spin
       on the opposite shore
               can speak
and the angle of your portrait
           projects
           (if i can face it)
    my own in me

iii

        i wear no necklace
                but feel the pull
the lunar clasp
        of perhaps
              one pearl, a tiny tusk
              dug-deep

its surge to surface
         met
            by the tap tap
                of infant palm
                on trunk
rooting for buried treasure
on the sea's lap

        Mother!
        why do you call me back?

iv

i received your smile with longing
like the bright coloured sweets
i loved to suck

        spacing them out
        on long cycle rides

           'how many miles to Harlow?'
           i practised division with pear drops

      the acid rests
           on the tongue-remembered way
to trickle
     trickle in
        the outline
            of the carmine kiss
forever
     plotted on the hanky
     hidden in my pocket

so, like an illusionist
i can whip it out
when everyone
will be amazed
how my smile bobs
like a buoy on the horizon

v

then dips

                oh how gently we
                go to sleep
                below the surface
                of the sea

could i
        could i
                become the beloved sun

        and rise again to round
        love's aureole, find land?

vi

M.   the music is muffled

                by ingrained sand

        i feel the scrape
        and sink

            touch sea-bed
            cut my teeth
            on empty oyster shells

drift
        nearly dilated
                my red sleeve streaming
                inside out

a ragged sea-urchin

there are no windows
at the bottom of the sea

> only bellies of fish
> an occasional glimmer
> the hulls of ships

>> with whom shall i sail?
>> didn't you see me ever?

floating past

> dressed for dinner
> in the land of table tops
> and gleaming silver

>> the carved breast

vii

i deliver my self

> out of the sea
> climb ashore
> and swing

>> in love's hammock
>> strung up
>> between two trees

where i play

> 'peep-bo'
> among the canvas folds

sing
and whistle

> for the child
> who was me

White Lilac
Phyllis Mansfield, 1914–1992

i face lilac in the early morning
find a child's voice

                answering back

in the lull
before the new day begins

i reply in two tones

             like my lilac facing
             one more pink
                the other quite blue

        have you ever looked at lilac?
        really looked at its frilly cones
        sketched against the sky

and felt it
      silent
            breathing in
            its short but fragrant dawn

beyond my sight
         there is another
                hidden
behind the cedar

        but right now
        i'm faced with lilac in two tones
        pink and blue

and the white can wait
while i hang out the washing

a certain harmony holds good
in my garden
set fair
      to meet the spring

and i have plenty of line
             a good length
between lilac and cedar
(though the last stretch under cedar is shady)

i love this lull in the early morning
when it is still quiet
                    and the world sleeps

there is time enough
                    to sort the load
                    (washing at night these days is cheaper)

enjoy the garden
                              and remember
                              mother's words about economy

                    'be sparing with pegs
                                        observe
                    the proper arrangement
                                             of linen on line
the right way to hang shirts
it's best to fold sheets'

men
        do you know of such things?

the daily changes in dress
marking our moods
                         our seasons

our growth charted by length
                                   and cut
the cloth itself
                 the way it hangs
                 displaying our relationship
                                        our inclination

i remember one year
when we girls
                    wore nothing but green
                    and men
                                nothing
                                    but grey

best of all i remember the babies' things

so tiny on the line
                 hardly
                 bigger than pegs
                                    all those cotton vests!

and my man
               do you understand now
               the time it takes?

this transformation
                    of amorphous bundles
                    to line
                              and back

do you respect
                    the small attentions
                              our delicacy?

why then
        don't you steal out
                         join me
in the lull surrounding
the mourning garden

pass me the pegs
               one by one

and i will tumble you
                          through words'
                          hidden meanings

if you
        will tumble me
                     just once more

complete
             our half-finished conversations
             in tones of pink and blue
                              then i
will go with you
                    beyond the winding sheets
                    behind the cedar

                         shall we seek
                         the white lilac?

Madonna del Parto
Piero della Francesca, (1412?–1492)

I think her eyes are sorrowful
and perplexed   the beautiful blue
of her dress parting like her hips
to allow the new life more room

how to make room when the stays
have been laced so tight for so long?
how to draw breath for two when all
around is new and she is filled to

the brim? how to drink eat make love
with joseph attend to the house
the family? where lies duty caught
between switchback angels who

fly between heaven and earth with
consummate ease? for she is flesh
as we are flesh and stand before

her knowing she came full term
and finally thank god found a room
to bear what we might only glimpse

Nightrain

Last night I slept with my window wide open
and woke up with the rain falling. Rain-air had
entered with the morning, merging somehow with
the dream of my return to the Island. I can still
hear the random patter of the raindrops and feel
their so certain downness.

Familiar shapes in the garden, the willow tree, fence,
even the blades of grass, now stand afresh, restored
to me by my dream and the rain falling. The rain
was like the dream; a gentle, continuous patter, patter,
patter, as though it had always been. And there was no
feeling of any inexorable ending to blight that sleep-
sunk state.

So it was that the rain-cloaked shapes from my garden
revealed themselves and dwelt with me awhile on the
Island. They fitted my dream like a glove and the
glove fitted me.

'The Avenue at Middelharnis'
after Meindert Hobbema (1638–1709)

Somewhere in this soil
lies part of me   the bones
which made me   decomposing
in an aura of graves
around my head

heed our dead   honour the living

so concentrated were we
round this place that *Koert*
blood colours the space
even between the trees
i see in the picture

their roots mine, mine theirs
if i am part tree woman, then
how is the human in tree?
our dead know
and somehow the poem

we know in our breathing

how our needs speak each
to each   creating balance
here there is no striving   only

surrender   as the bows
of ships   whose masts i see
surrender to the water

where we all once were   so
small in our first salt garden
where we swam   sifted destiny
through gills   grew spines

Brotherhood

i

The city smells sour.
No chimneys smoking
blood into the hearth.
No eats, provoking

scrums on the cold
street corner. I'm
at Waterloo in con-
versation with a mime

of my exiled brother
in Frisco. He owns
a restaurant serving
real food he grows

himself. He opened up
when Dad passed away,
thinking he could go it
alone. Now the day

has come to sit round
the table. Take off
our time worn disguises
donned to scoff...

ii

Regard the sister, who
still in her shift, hides
inside a suit's high
fashion casing. Cried

out eyes stare dry
and, sat on her butt
the shrivelled fruit
lies wasting. In a rut

for years and hating
the white slaver
which wolfs her silver,
eviscerating to lather

its own appetite. I
need to find a way
to clinch this final
rout. Or, before day

it will blow my soul,
sucked out by fangs
between butterfly lips
to pupate in pangs

of surrogacy.

iii

my mum took me out
to buy me my first ski suit
when we went to the snow
many years ago

i loved this suit so much
no one else
had anything quite like it

it was all red
with a hood to match
which would draw tight
round my face and
keep the wind out

looking at old photos
now i can see how
i looked so strange
with my tiny face
in dark glasses, framed
by a drawstring,
against the glare

a regular hood

iv

i would do anything
for you my brother
if only you knew

how i loved
those descents
quite out of control

with me always up front
you devil   always ready
for me to take the rap

me   only half your size
red against the white
snow and you in black

how that sledge moved!

when we couldn't make
the bend it was i
who shot off smack
head first in the high
banks of snow

i was your brake
a willing accomplice
and ready to take it all

ready to take it all

v

the ascents were different
in those drag lift days i was so
light   the button between my legs
was drawn too tight
the tension wrong
for an intrepid skier
so slight

fear was already
no stranger   nor separation
they held for me
a strange fascination

an outrageous flirtation
with jaws gaping
like the huge ravine
spread-eagled
beneath me

i was in the air
skis out of control
suspended over that bridge

the button between my legs
was drawn too tight
the tension wrong
for an intrepid skier
so slight

vi

that night i had trouble
breathing
dad said you'd been winding
me up   we'd fought

you   twice my size
the odds always seemed
against me

i donned my dark glasses
and pulled the drawstring
tight against your glare

avoiding the light
i breathed in danger
that night

you saw through
the little red hood
you knew i'd done this
to spite you

to spite you
i learned how to dance
through life   the tension tight
so used to a life of danger

vii

it separated us
as deftly as you crack
eggs against the china bowl

but you were the yoke
to my white slaver
on painted butterfly lips

OK let's call it quits...

my whole body weeps on to the track
its silver glancing from left
to right under the station dome

as we move off i gather it up
and the points shift
the points shift

III

Free Association with Raging Bull
Yellow Canary shoots E. Pistol'Ary

Shoot! Opening bars
by the pool   Picked up
Serenade then fuck

Walk down aisle
The usual beat
Usual tweet

Exchange of rings
Choke on the vow
Blonde holy cow

breeds   Rare steak
fed for lunch
Dance   then punch

Frees Fist thrust deep
into basin of ice
Womb numbed life

licked into shape
Tongue tied
Gloved sacrifice

Sparring become altar
Bereaved flesh
Cunt damp dress

Splice Bob is Jake
is Brando is me
mirrored iconography

On the rocks
Neat blood speech
Liquid peace

Credits   My life
is starring me! Laughter
mother to daughter

vinyl bandage

at the last he set us
to work on the collection
a lifetime of 'wants'
lined our walls, a vast
vinyl bandage, his wealth

how many times had i sat
on the sofa pleading health!
still colossal in his chair, he
resisted, blind, until the
tumour, like a worm

in the bud, began to eat its
way out and let the light in.
too late! my own colossus
corralled, i knelt at his feet,
our daughters beside me

obedient to his instructions
we graded and priced each
disc during three whole weeks
of his time remaining all we
had ever wanted was 'home'

and 'home' we had …

Anatomy of Loss

Christmas approaches and
my body aches in all
the places your jewellery
used to touch, illuminate.

Those mineral initials
chosen in my absence –
extravagant tokens
bought to satisfy

an ambiguous lust
for ownership and self-
esteem your flesh
denied you. Where was I

among the ranked collections,
the unopened thrillers,
cellophaned cds, the books
of unstruck matches mapping

the trade route of buying
expeditions? From east to
west your hands roamed,
driven by a feeling eye.

Its doomed navel ignition
sparked a whole culture of
collecting plundering the
family purse, and which leaves me

alone atop the Christmas tree.
Spectacled – peering through
holes left by your missing stones,
feeling for a magic wand, alive.

Time has come

I

Time has come
Between us.
Your still warm
Corpse pressed in
To new space.
Your new born
Face smooth. Its
Folds fallen
Away from
Creases I
Helped to make.

II

The house shifts.
Our children
Wait on my
Hands to knead
Dough of un-
Knowing, to
Shape bread for
Your wake. Numb,
I am half
Gone with you
In Hades.

III

My season
In Hell. Laid
Out like a
Whore on a
Hot bed, I
made out with
My own dung.
Dumb, it was
Only the
Cunt which spoke.
Saw our life's

IV

Foliage shed
Leaf by leaf.
Fall – ding, dong
Dell – down my
Own well of
Knowing. My
Gorgon time.
Both spider
And fly caught
In a spin.
Survival

V

Eyeing up
Its chances.
Pity the
Poor sod who
Came. Planted
His seed in
That horny
Place thinking
Pleasure! God
Fear the bite
Of Nature.

VI

Her other
Face no less
A gift than
Flowers' chaste
Flirting with
Bees, honey
Bound. God fear
The action
When we hit
Rock bottom.
Find the tap

VII

Root rotten.
The well dry.
How to speak
In season
With myself?
Tell? How he,
Our Mister
D, Mister
Shit of Cen-
Turies took
A rise on

VIII

Me. Rode me
Up and out.
That power
House spouting
Laughter. Backed
Me. Brought to
A head that
Bud of black-
Ness. Out of
Split sides new
Life sprouted.

IV

birth day
(in mesopotamia)

i

truth sits like a swallow
on my branches   come winter
                                        migrates

africa comes close
i can almost smell her
sadness at the foot of the stairs
i hesitate   hear the cry
of wild animals   feel their footfalls
through the flimsy partition

listen   light my candle
they are coming up to feed   ancestors
from the river   where the euphrates flows
my sap is resinous   i am distant
and the winged bull posts
at the four-headed gate

ii

split-level life   love
                    on the wing
                    reader   be my lover
discover with me
the lost language of trees

                            recover
root talk   trunk talk   talk
defined by weather   and the turning
leaves   bind us together
                            in dream
you spoke of ecclesiastes

how the root palace seethes
                    under stars

iii

the sum of your years
spreads out like a map on the table
there is the jug   the wine
i drink   break bread with you
tell me   where have you been
between the points of time's compass?

ride with me   due east   on the back
of the evening sky   round the quarters
clouded in dapples of grey and white
(only truth could bear such beauty)
so take me from behind   ride pillion
we rhyme
                quick   catch up the reins
           spring
                in the saddle
                                  inlaid
                                  with moonlight

darling   the sun rises
                               how time flies

UR

intent
as a huddle
of men
rolling
dice
on life's
street
corner
so
the game
slips by

and
prize
live cargo
changes
into tombs

fugitive

i

                    dawn
the black silk surrounding
sloughs off
snake-skin of night slewn
by licorice columns of fear
sucked dry
and i fade
pale
as the moon's membrane
into the day's mouth

                    i had
the pick of fine things
the girl whom everyone knows
recognises
my hair already reaches
(well nearly) to my knees
and i often wear it loose
for my father the king

and for whom
it is now tightly braided
in coils

i will not go with him!
my skin is not grey
like the drained ditch
in winter   mine
is the delta in spring

ii

                the guard
silently paces
i dip the licorice stick
a last time into sherbet
stifle the fizz on my tongue
quench my sparkle   sneeze

change into another's things
i am sinuous   tubular
with a quick flick
i tail my defiance
poke my tongue
glide past the guard
out in to the palace garden
and make for the delta

hug the ground
scale the gate
pause
peek over
get
my bearings

slide
belly down
over the top

down
down
in
to
the
delta

iii

my licorice stick

the familiar found
in an alien place
where yesterday re-
turns to root today

in love?
in hate?
    how
           do they taste?
    how
           do they touch?

i start to suck
search the hidden
crevices with my tongue

milk life at the source
its limb growing strong
within we are fibrous
we fray our maiden
heads surrender in
play draw blood

new language nipped
in the bud?

iv

post – bolt

passed from hand to
hand   graded 'first'
traded in   peeped
at behind pillars
tossed off   say
the dog 'fetch' and
he will run unravel
me on his soft tongue
pant at his mistress's
pleasure – answers
in a soft scream
of scissors' stroke
sheer to the gullet
now   feel how my
kingdom unfolds
from within – 'come'

History of a Lost Umbrella

there are no crowds flowing
over this London bridge

just we two

i, in my alpaca coat
silk scarf

and he, in his dark duffle
of navy blue
padded out against the cold
a burly figure, big
but not through feeding

he caught my eye
swigging the dregs
the likes of us leave
i saw him swill
the bitter crescent of lemon
round   then look at me

we left the National
together, found ourselves
beside the river
linked by a glinting core of steel

the skeleton of a lost umbrella

its naked shaft riveting
my attention
as he twirled it round and round
like a crazy knight giving
a dazed display of swordsmanship

II

I am the shaft
speaking
through which we fall
dreaming
The very same sword
drawn from the stone
Patroklus parried me
straight
standing for Achilles
his brother
Homer who penned me
handed me over
mutable as the river
flowing toward the sea
So I feed into
the outstretched hand
cupped in the land
of imagination
thirsting
for trade in life's
hand-me-downs
with this simple history
of a lost umbrella

III

i sing now, as patroklus
sang, in the name of poetry
my brother   hear my song!
lend me your armour
your cloaked tongue
in which i may steal out
into the night and enter
the back door of men's hearts
while they lie naked, sleeping
shields down   i'll mend
the torn fabric of lives
shuffled by the wolf pack
gorging on fear, stalked

quietly and in secret
i will sew and sing, recover
the dark fragments thrown
and with a woman's deft hands
fashion anew the separate
strands into bright domes
both 'parasol' and 'parapluie'
with all the fantasy and care
of a woman who loves

IV

Found, I stripped it
of the fabric, chucked it
with my man's hard throw
and arched back
With my head thrown back
I threw that crumpled ball
of synthetic black as though
it were a javelin
far out, over the river
I saw it open out
like a parachute
lit by the city light
and remembered me the fires
as we flew over after the drop
It began to fall but the breeze
took it, carried it right out
and blimey, as it flew I fancy
it changed, fell like a falling
star in a swanky black ballgown
Down, into the river

V

That throw came back
when I saw her there
just as I bit
into the bitter crescent
of another man's lemon
My tongue furled like a flag
on the tartness

I saw her, saw her sweep
down the stair in a great coat
but dainty, I swear
underneath
Like a fabulous bird, nesting

I know she saw me stare
Before I knew it we were
outside together
Me feinting at the parked
limousines to hide my confusion

VI

tremulous
with only the sky's sheath
for protection
i engaged
the man in conversation
trod the walkway
of his desire
honed like a blade
by war and isolation

i told him
my name
but his
he said, was guarded

he said he was
a hundred thousand strong
alone on a bench at night
and all the time
the naked core was glinting
as he danced from left to right

we climbed the steps
on to the bridge
the barrier was so low
and i felt his fear at bay
alongside me
its hollow vessel hungry

and the pull
of deep water
down my throat

VII

from his hand i flew
felt the breeze lift me
oh how it hurts to be apart
from the bone and sinew
which first shaped me, gave
me my form and regal station
held by kings in palanquins
i shaded the heads of queens

now i am made so plainly
my saving grace the strength
of my fabric
i am black
synthetic and tough

i hang
from this buttress
where the wind took me
and wait patiently
while the river tells me
all her secrets and long
enough for those above to love
again and clothe my core
in silk brocade and deep fringes

fear will have no home
under my re-furbished dome
where poetry, in brotherhood
will reign

Notes to the poems

Life Palette 'O sol é grande; caem co'a calma as aves' Sá de Miranda (1481–1558) Portuguese renaissance poet The sun is high; birds swoop in the stillness (the author's translation)

lollipop 'Psameadd' is the sand fairy in E. Nesbit's novel *Five Children and It.* 'Wanderer' is an Old English poem preserved only in an anthology known as the Exeter Book, a manuscript dating from the late 10th century. Two of its principal themes are exile and the search for wisdom in the face of adversity.

Pointer The object in question is the 'Alfred Jewel', a pointer, or aestel, (in the form of a dog's snout) and was commissioned by Alfred the Great. It is believed to have been used to follow the text in a gospel book and is housed in the Ashmolean museum, Oxford.

A *burh* is an Old English name for a fortified town or other defended site, sometimes centred upon a hill fort

The Ballad of Zé and Marie The choice of Vigo, a coastal town in Galicia, is not arbitrary in that it was the topos for many beautiful lyrics in the medieval poetry tradition of the *cantigas de amigo*

diaspora The quotation is from Vicki Feaver's poem 'The Avenue at Middelharnis' in her collection (1994) *The Handless Maiden*

The Dutch and Dentists 'The seventeenth century Dutch were perhaps the first to pay for their unprecedented prosperity with their teeth!' Harvey and Sheldon Peck, orthodontists, Discover, October 1980 (from Simon Schama's *The Embarrassment of Riches – an interpretation of Dutch culture in the Golden Age.*

for Serge Gainsbourg Serge Gainsbourg (1928–1991) was a multi-talented French poet and composer of Russian Jewish origin. Among his many talents, including that of 'provocateur', he was also an accomplished painter and pianist. In his early life he struggled to

85

overcome extreme shyness and what he considered to be his physical unattractiveness.

The Avenue at Middelharnis The painting referred to may be seen in London's National Gallery which (according to my uncle) was bought from the town council in Middelharnis for two hundred florins. Its innovativeness was unappreciated at the time of its painting and Hobbema was unable to make a living from his art. My father was brought up very close to the avenue in question; the view it affords has hardly changed. A striking work where the earth's atmosphere is one of the principal components of its composition.

Free Association with Raging Bull The film *Raging Bull* (1980) directed by Martin Scorsese is a biopic of the boxer Jake LaMotta, and stars Robert de Niro as Jake LaMotta. It is considered by critics to be the best film of that decade. Scorsese incorporates a reference in the screenplay to the film On the *Waterfront* (1954), starring Marlon Brando, with the famous quote 'I coulda been a contender'.

Acknowledgements

Madonna del Parto was first published in the pamphlet 'Switchback Angels' Leni Dipple – Priapus Press, editor John Cotton in 1994

left-handed appeared in issue 7 (1998) of the magazine *Interpreter's House*

Perspective with Matisse was published by the Ware Poets group in 1997

Thanks to:

Ion Mills for his support and friendship in bringing these poems into the light

Ellen Phethean for accompanying me on the journey and for her valuable editorial insights

Willem Koert (1922–2013) for translating his father's correspondence to Sara Gnirrep

Helder Macedo inspired poet and teacher; always a confirming presence of the best life can offer

Leni and Pierre Cauvin for their *joie de vivre*, their love and support

Graham Griffiths for his invaluable contribution in the making of Mole Jazz

Nigel Scott for the support he gave to my late husband and his presence in the Mole Jazz years

Iul – Lassiters Cafe for a decade of making me feel welcome in exchange for a cappucino

Didier Mathieu Director of Le Centre des livres d'artistes, St. Yrieix La Perche – for his cover design and way-in to a new creative partnership

About Us

Oldcastle Books has a number of other imprints, including
No Exit Press, Kamera Books, Creative Essentials,
Pulp! The Classics, Pocket Essentials and High Stakes
Publishing > oldcastlebooks.co.uk

For more information about Crime Books go to >
crimetime.co.uk

Check out the kamera film salon for independent,
arthouse and world cinema > kamera.co.uk

For more information, media enquiries and review copies
please contact Frances
> frances@oldcastlebooks.com